The Tiny Gardeners

Kat Macleod

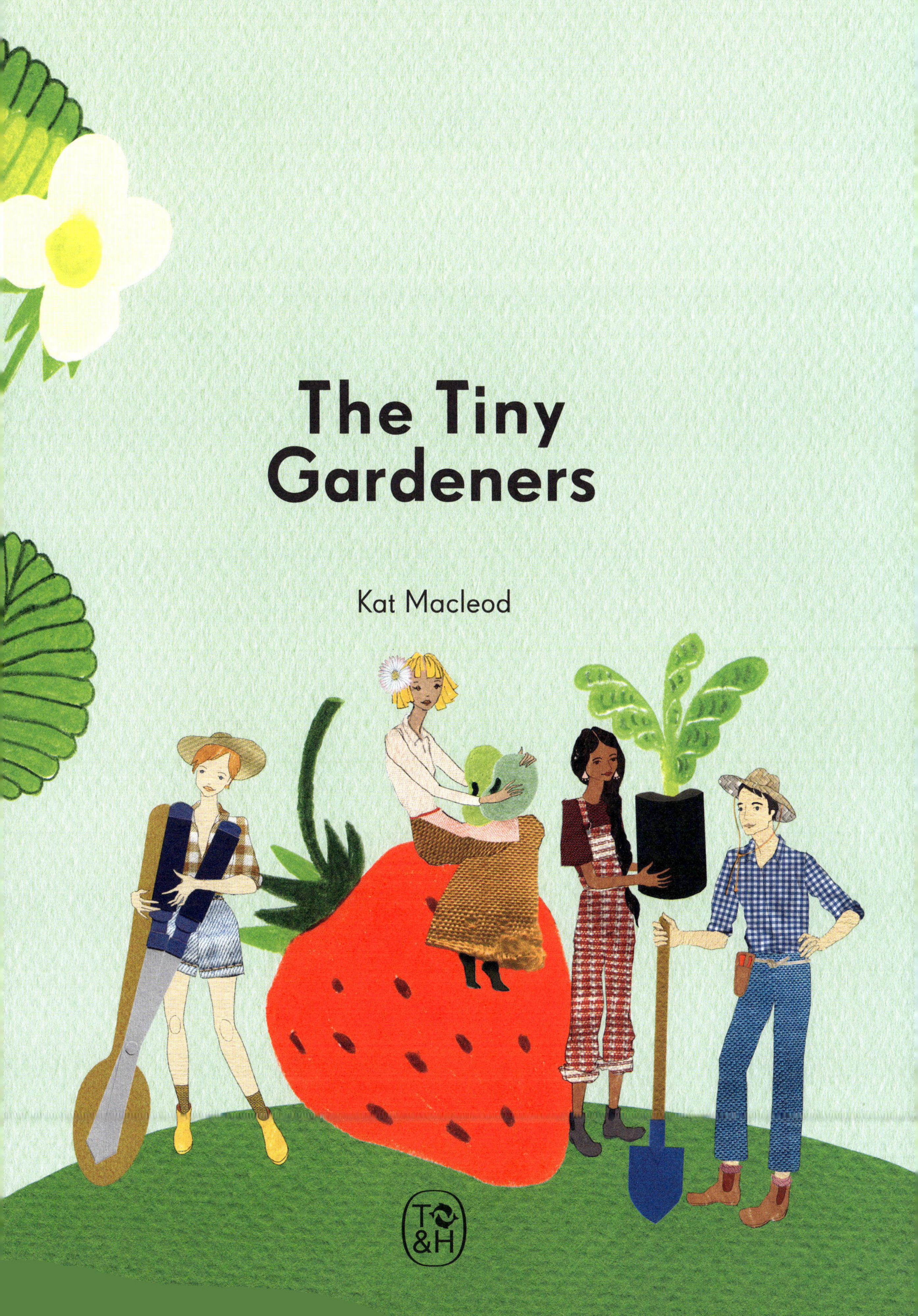

It's a clear, brisk
morning in the garden.

The sun is getting warmer and
it's time for a new growing season.
Who looks after this promising patch?

The Tiny Gardeners!
Here they are, ready
with their tools.

They tend to the plants
and harvest the produce
in time for the Summer Market.

It takes a lot of care to grow a garden. Let's have a look ...

Out in the vegetable plot,
preparation begins.

Turning the soil ...

Pressing seeds gently
into the earth ...

Lining up stakes
for plants to climb.

In time, the
vegetables will grow.

Over in the fruit patch, preparation begins.

Scattering seeds ...

Planting berry canes ...

Checking on new buds
high up in the tree.

In time, the
fruit will grow.

Deep in the herb garden,
preparation begins.

Potting seeds from
last year's crop ...

Transplanting cuttings that
will soon become bushes ...

Choosing a sunny spot for new shoots.

In time, the herbs will grow.

Down in the flower bed,
preparation begins.

Pruning old branches
and dead ends ...

Carefully mulching
around the roots ...

Tugging out weeds to
keep the garden tidy.

In time, the
flowers will grow.

All around the garden ...

Bees buzz from flower to flower, spreading pollen to help the plants flourish.

Time passes and the garden is growing. Let's have a look ...

Wow!

What can you see?

Long, bumpy beans.

Shiny, round tomatoes.

Bright pink radishes.

It’s nearly time to harvest
on this hot and humid day ...

The vegetables are thirsty!

Yum!

What can you taste?

Fresh, juicy strawberries.

Tart, zingy blackberries.

Sweet, tropical mangoes.

It's nearly time to harvest
on this hot and humid day ...

The fruit is drooping!

Ooooh!

What can you touch and feel?

Rough, pebbly mint leaves.

Spiky rosemary sprigs.

Jagged-edged parsley.

It's nearly time to harvest
on this hot and humid day ...

The herbs are shrivelling!

Mmmmm!

What can you smell?

Rich-scented roses.

Calming lavender perfume.

Sweetly fragrant honeysuckle.

It's nearly time to harvest
on this hot and humid day ...

The flowers are wilting!

Listen!

The insects are busy.
What can you hear?

Humming, hovering bees.

Scuttling, scampering ladybirds.

Shrilling, chattering cicadas.

It's nearly harvest time on this hot and humid day, and the sun has disappeared.

Just a moment, what's that new sound?

Rumble
Crack

Flash
BOOM!

The storm ends and the sun shines. Finally, it's harvest time!

The Tiny Gardeners snip, chop, pick and collect everything they need from their well-watered garden.

Right.

On.

Time.

Look at everything the Tiny Gardeners have grown.

A delicious feast for the senses!

M A R K E T
HERBS 1.29
ROSES 1.99
HONEYSUCKLE 0.20
LAVENDER 0.15
TOMATOES 0.50

For my mum and dad,
and the gardens they grow.

Big thanks to Kirsten Abbott, Kristin Gill, Lisa Schuurman and Natasha Grogan.

Kat Macleod is an illustrator, designer and exhibiting artist. She is endlessly inspired by nature, fashion and textiles, and the drawings of her three young boys.

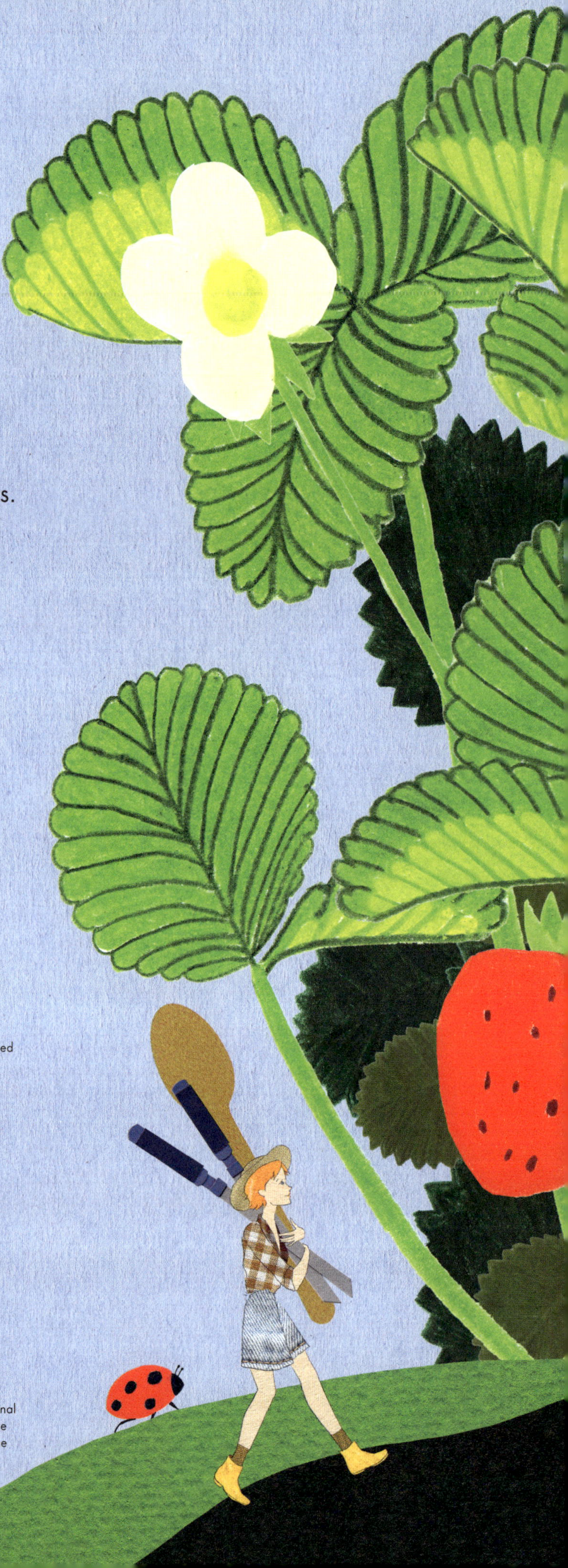

First published in Australia in 2024
by Thames & Hudson Australia
Wurundjeri Country
132A Gwynne Street
Cremorne, Victoria 3121

27 26 25 24 5 4 3 2 1

ISBN 978-1-760-76336-7

A catalogue record for this book is available from the National Library of Australia

Design: Kat Macleod
Printed and bound in China
by 1010 Printing International Limited

Thames & Hudson Australia and the author wish to acknowledge that Aboriginal and Torres Strait Islander peoples are the first storytellers of this nation and the Traditional Custodians of the land on which we live and work. We acknowledge their continuing culture and pay respect to Elders past and present.

thamesandhudson.com.au

Kat Macleod